The Bogeyman Caper

The Bogeyman Caper

by Susan Pearson

illustrated by Gioia Fiammenghi

SIMON AND SCHUSTER BOOKS FOR YOUNG READERS

PUBLISHED BY SIMON & SCHUSTER INC.

New York • London • Toronto • Sydney • Tokyo • Singapore

For Jane Resh Thomas,
lighter of sparks—SP

To Laura—GF

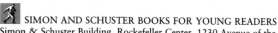
SIMON AND SCHUSTER BOOKS FOR YOUNG READERS
Simon & Schuster Building, Rockefeller Center, 1230 Avenue of the Americas, New York,
New York 10020. Text copyright © 1990 by Susan Pearson. Illustrations copyright © 1990
by Gioia Fiammenghi. All rights reserved including the right of reproduction in whole or
in part in any form. SIMON AND SCHUSTER BOOKS FOR YOUNG READERS is a trademark of
Simon & Schuster Inc.
Designed by Lucille Chomowicz
Manufactured in the United States of America
10 9 8 7 6 5 4 3 2 1   pbk. 10 9 8 7 6 5 4 3 2 1
Library of Congress Cataloging-in-Publication Data: Pearson, Susan. The bogeyman caper.
Summary: When the kids at school tell her that an old house is haunted by a bogeyman,
Ernie uses her "eagle eye" to prove them wrong. [1. Mystery and detective stories. 2. Haunted
houses—Fiction. 3. Schools—Fiction.] I. Fiammenghi, Gioia, ill. II. Title.
PZ7.P323316Bo 1990 [Fic]—dc20   89-26211
ISBN 0-671-70565-2   ISBN 0-671-70569-5 (pbk.)

CONTENTS

CHAPTER 1

The Old Yellow House

"A bogeyman lives in that house," said William.

"That's silly," said Ernie.

"He's right," said R.T. R.T.'s real name was Rachel, but everyone called her R.T. She twisted one of her braids around her finger. Then she began to chew on it. "That's why no one ever goes there on Halloween."

"Or ever cuts through that yard," added Michael.

"I thought you were listening to Mission Control," said Ernie

"I was," said Michael. He took his big headphones off his ears. He hung them around his neck. "This is more interesting," he said. "Nothing much is going on in space today."

The four friends were walking home from school. They were taking the long cut. It was a sunny October afternoon. Leaves were everywhere.

Ernie scuffed her feet. She kicked the leaves. Little clouds of dust rose up around them.

Ernie didn't think she believed in bogeymen. "There's no such thing as a bogeyman," she said.

"Is too," said Michael. "Just cut through that yard. You'll find out."

"How do you know?" asked Ernie.

"Everybody knows," said Michael.

"He eats puppies and rabbits and squirrels and stuff," said R.T. "I never bring Ralph near here." Ralph was R.T.'s rabbit.

"He cooks them like hot dogs on a stick," said Michael. "Get it? Hot Dogs! Ha, ha, ha. Sometimes you can see his fire."

2

Michael was marching. One foot marched on the sidewalk. One foot marched in the street leaves.

"My brother went up to the window once," he said. He lowered his voice. "He heard all kinds of weird stuff. Moans and groans. Dogs howling. *Hoooooooooooooo.*" Michael made his voice jiggle.

"Did anyone ever see him?" asked Ernie.

"Course not!" Michael snorted. "No one ever sees a bogeyman."

"No one ever sees him because he isn't there," said Ernie. "Even if there are bogeymen, they don't live in White Bear Lake."

"Where do they live, then?" asked Michael. "Newport News?"

Ernie had lived in Newport News, Virginia, before she moved to White Bear Lake, Minnesota.

"Not there, either," said Ernie. "Transylvania maybe. But they don't live in White Bear Lake."

"Do too," said Michael.

"Do not," said Ernie.

"Do too," said Michael and R.T. and William.

"I saw him," said William.

Everyone stopped. They all stared at William.

"Well, I did," said William. "He changes into a dog sometimes. I saw him in back of my house once. He tipped over our garbage can. My dad called the pound. But he got away."

"Of course," said R.T. "He changed back into a man. Bogeymen can do that, you know."

She pointed to the old yellow house. A scrawny orange cat was sleeping on the porch. One of its ears looked chewed up. It had a bald spot on its head.

"That's probably him right there," she whispered, "listening to every word we say. Just waiting for us to go into his yard."

R.T. looked at them. She was chewing her braid like crazy. Suddenly, she spit it out and ran down the street. Michael ran after her. They turned the corner. They kept on running.

"Come on, Ernie!" shouted William. He ran to the corner. Then he stopped for a second. He looked back at Ernie.

"Hurry up!" he begged, "before he gets you." Then he ran after Michael and R.T.

Ernie did not run. That old cat didn't look very dangerous to her. It looked tired out. Besides, she should take a good look. After all, she had an eagle eye. Maybe she would see something important—something to prove there was no bogeyman.

It looked like just any old house, kind of big and sprawly. It needed paint. Its yellow color looked dirty.

There was a giant tree in the yard to the left of the house. Behind it was a garage. Near the garage was a garden. The lawn was all covered with leaves, but the garden was tidy. There were no plants in it now, just dirt.

Ernie looked back at the house. It had a big front porch. The porch had a swing. One of its chains was broken. One side of the swing was up in the air. The other side was on the floor. The shutters were all crooked.

Ernie thought the house looked sad.

Two front windows were wide open. The curtains were blowing inside. Ernie thought about that. A bogeyman wouldn't have curtains. And he wouldn't leave his windows open. She was sure of it.

Suddenly, the cat stood up. It stretched and yawned. Its mouth was huge! It had about a hundred teeth! One of its yellow eyes stared right at Ernie. The other one stayed shut.

Ernie froze. She stared right back. She couldn't help it.

Finally, the cat turned its head. It walked across the porch. It jumped through a window. Then it disappeared.

Ernie's tummy flip-flopped. She raced around the corner after her friends.

CHAPTER 2

Two Disguises

Ernie thought about the bogeyman all night long.

She checked all her books. She didn't find one bogeyman.

She did find lots of witches, a few giants, two brownies, and five ghosts. All of them lived in faraway places. Most of them lived in Once-upon-a-time. Not one of them lived in Minnesota.

Ernie was angry with herself. That orange cat was just a cat. She should not have been afraid of it. There was no bogeyman in that house. Tomorrow she would prove it!

*   *   *

"Good morning, lamb," said Mommy. "What would you like for breakfast?"

"Brain food," said Ernie.

"Fish is brain food," said Mommy. "Do you want fish for breakfast?"

"Yuck," said Ernie. "I don't need to be that brainy."

"I think bananas are brain food," said Mommy. "How about banana pancakes?"

"Yummy," said Ernie. "Can I mash the bananas?"

"Sure," said Mommy. She handed Ernie the potato masher and a bowl and three bananas.

Ernie got right to work. *Mash, mash, mash.* She could feel her brain getting smarter already.

First she needed some disguises. She thought about the tree in the bogeyman's yard. A tree would be good, but a tree was too hard to make. Maybe she could make a little tree. Or a bush. That was it!

"Mommy," she said. "You know those

pretend branches you hang on the stairs at Christmas?"

"You mean the garlands?" said Mommy.

Ernie nodded. "Can I borrow one?"

"What for?" asked Mommy.

"I need to build a bush," Ernie explained.

"I guess that would be all right," said Mommy. "Just promise not to cut it."

Ernie promised.

"They are in the attic," said Mommy. "I'll get one after breakfast."

That took care of one disguise. Now Ernie needed one more. One for her. She thought up that one while she ate her pancakes. Those bananas were good brain food.

After breakfast, Ernie went to her closet. She pulled out her dress-up box. Inside was a big ball of yellow yarn. She knew she had saved it for something.

Ernie wound the yarn around her chair— five times, ten times, fifteen times, twenty times, twenty-five times. Then she ran out of yarn. She hoped it was enough.

9

She slid the loop of yarn off the chair. Next she tied a little piece of yarn around the middle of the loop. Then she cut the ends of the loop.

She shook the yarn out. It looked like a giant pom-pom. She plopped it on her head. Hmmmm.

Ernie took the wig off. She cut some of the yarn to make bangs. Then she tried it on again. Perfect! She looked just like that awful Marcie at school. Well, almost. She didn't smell like Juicy Fruit gum. But nobody was going to smell her, anyway.

Ernie ran to the basement. She found an old magazine. She took it back to her room. Ernie glued a few pages to the back cover. She let the glue dry. Then she cut a hole through the glued pages.

She was ready. There was just one thing left to do. Talk William into this!

CHAPTER 3

The Martian Club

William and R.T. and Michael were all in Michael's backyard. They were in the *Star Finder*. The *Star Finder* was Michael's spaceship. A sign on the door said:

STAR FINDER
Travel through Space
with Commander Michael

The *Star Finder* was really an old playhouse. Michael had one big brother and three big sisters. His brother was in high school. His sisters were big, too. Sometimes Julia baby-sat Ernie. The playhouse was theirs. They didn't use it anymore, though. Now it was Michael's.

The *Star Finder* was also the Martian clubhouse. Another sign on the door said:

MARTIAN CLUB
PRIVATE!
MARTIANS ONLY!
THIS MEANS
PRINCE MICHAEL
QUEEN ERNIE
KING WILLIAM
QUEEN R.T.
EVERYONE ELSE KEEP OUT!

Today Michael was planning a trip to Jupiter. William and R.T. were his crew. They were all sitting on orange crates.

R.T. was holding Ralph in her lap. Ralph was her rabbit. She was feeding him bits of lettuce. R.T. always had lettuce in her pocket.

William was drawing Ralph's picture. "Hold him still," he told R.T.

Michael had on his headphones. He was talking to Mission Control.

"They need a piano on Jupiter," he said, "and a piano player—that's me. And two elephants. And one rabbit. And a vet—that's you, R.T."

"What about me?" asked William.

"I have a mission for you," said Ernie, "but it's not on Jupiter. It's right here on Earth."

"What is it?" asked William.

"Can we come too?" asked R.T.

"Tell us," said Michael.

Ernie tried to sound like Mission Control. "This is a Top Secret Mission," she said, "for Top Secret Spies. We will go where no man has gone before. We will prove that there is no bogeyman."

"But there *is* a bogeyman," said Michael.

"In the old yellow house," said R.T.

William didn't say a word.

"You don't know that," said Ernie. She told them about the disguises. "I will watch the front of the house," she said, "through the magazine. William will watch the back through the bush."

"You will get killed," said R.T.

"And cooked like a hot dog," said Michael.

William still didn't say a word.

"No we won't," said Ernie. "There is no bogeyman in that house. And anyway, we will be wearing disguises."

"I'm not going," said Michael.

"Me neither," said R.T.

William didn't say anything.

"That's why I'm taking William," said Ernie. "Only the bravest can go on this mission. Only a Martian king."

Now nobody said a word. Everybody stared at William.

William stood on one foot. Then he stood on the other foot. Then he looked at the floor. Then he looked at Ernie. Finally, he opened his mouth.

"I'll do it!" he said.

"Hooray!" shouted Ernie. "I knew you were brave, William!"

William grinned.

"Hooray for William!" shouted Michael.

"Hooray for King William," shouted R.T., "king of the Martian Club!"

They both looked glad that they were not going.

"We will help you get ready," said Michael.

"I am already ready," said Ernie.

"No, you're not," said Michael. "How will you report to each other? You can't just shout across the yard. You need a walkie-talkie."

"You are right," said Ernie. "Do you have one?"

"No," said Michael, "but I know how to make one."

"What about food?" said R.T. "You may be there a long time."

"Good idea!" said Ernie.

16

Michael went into his house. He came out with a bag. He set it on an orange crate. Then he unpacked it. There was:

1 ball of nylon string
2 paper cups
1 box of toothpicks
1 loaf of bread
1 jar of peanut butter
1 bag of cookies
1 knife
1 pair of scissors

The Martians got right to work. King William and Queen R.T. made sandwiches. Prince Michael showed Queen Ernie how to make a walkie-talkie.

First he took a toothpick. He punched a hole in the bottom of each paper cup. Then he stuck the string through the bottom of one of the cups. He tied the string to a tooth-pick. Next he cut off the ends of the tooth-pick so it would lay flat in the cup.

"Hold this," he told Ernie.

Ernie held the cup.

Michael picked up the ball of string. He walked out the door. He walked across the backyard. He walked all the way to the front of his house. Then he turned around and walked back.

"This should be enough string," he said. He cut it off the ball. Then he stuck it through the bottom of the other cup. He tied it to another toothpick. He cut off the ends of that toothpick.

"Let's try it out," said Ernie.

"Okay," said Michael. "You stand by the garage. I'll stand at the end of the driveway."

They took their places.

"You have to hold the string tight," Michael yelled. "And it can't touch anything."

Ernie held her cup to her mouth. Michael held his by his ear.

"Calling Prince Michael," Ernie said into the cup. "Prince Michael, come in." She held her cup next to her ear.

"Roger. Commander Michael here."

Michael's voice came through loud and clear. The walkie-talkie worked!

William and R.T. wanted to try it. Then William wanted to try it with Ernie. Then R.T. wanted to try it with Michael.

Finally, everyone had tried it with everyone. They all went back inside the *Star Finder*.

"When will you go?" Michael asked.

"Tomorrow afternoon," said Ernie. "Okay, William?"

"Roger," said William.

"Meet here at three o'clock," said Ernie.

"Roger," said William again.

R.T. reached into her pocket—the one without the lettuce. She pulled out a little rubber rabbit. It had a metal ring stuck into its head.

"This is my good luck piece," she said. "It used to have a chain to hang around your neck." R.T. handed the rabbit to William. "You can have this," she said.

"For keeps?" said William.

"For keeps," said R.T.

Then Michael opened the bag of cookies. It was half empty. They ate all the cookies that were left.

CHAPTER 4

Top Secret Spies

It was Sunday afternoon. Ernie was ready. She picked up her shopping bag. Everything she needed was in it:

> the Christmas garland
> the magazine with the hole
> the yarn wig
> bobby pins
> big safety pins
> an old rubber poncho

The rubber poncho had some holes in it. Daddy had thrown it away. Today Ernie was glad she had saved it.

William had the walkie-talkie and the sandwiches.

Ernie walked to the *Star Finder*. Michael and R.T. and William were already there. Today it had a new sign on the door:

SPY HQ

William was wearing his rabbit. It was on a string around his neck.

Ernie put on her wig. She pinned it to her hair.

R.T. giggled. "You look like Marcie," she said, "but you don't smell like Juicy Fruit."

Then everyone helped dress William.

"Hold this on your head," said Ernie. She handed William one end of the garland. William held it on his head.

Then Ernie marched around William. Around and around and around, until he was all wrapped up in garland.

R.T. pinned the garland to William's hair. Michael and Ernie pinned it to William's clothes. Then they all stood back to look.

"Wow!" said R.T. "You look great, William."

"Just like a bush," said Ernie.

"Or a short Christmas tree," said Michael.

"Really?" said William. "I wish I could see me."

Ernie dropped the poncho over William's head. She pulled up the hood.

"Spies have to be secret," she said. "You can't walk up the street looking like a bush. Bushes can't walk!"

William put the sandwiches into one poncho pocket. He put the walkie-talkie into the other.

Ernie picked up her magazine. "Let's go!" she said. She hoped she sounded brave. She didn't believe in bogeymen, but her tummy flip-flopped anyway.

"We'd better go with you," said Michael.

"We can help you get set up," said R.T.

Ernie felt a little braver.

The four friends walked to the yellow house. They stood across the street.

Ernie pulled off William's poncho. She handed him a sandwich. She handed him one end of the walkie-talkie.

"Your place is next to the big tree," she said. "You can see the backyard from there. And the garage. And the garden."

"You mean, in the yard?" William whispered.

"You can hide behind the tree," said Ernie.

William's branches began to shake. Ernie heard him swallow. But he didn't say anything. He looked both ways. He crossed the street. Then he ran to the tree.

R.T. was chewing on both her braids. Michael was quiet for once.

There was a stone wall behind Ernie. She sat down on it. She picked up her magazine. She pretended to read it, but she wasn't

reading. She was looking through the hole.

She could see the yard. She could see the side of the garage. She could see the garden. She could see the tree. She could see William the bush.

She could see the whole front of the house. The windows were still open. The orange cat jumped out of one. Its eye was still shut. And it had a stiff leg today, too. It limped to the top of the steps. It stretched out in the sun.

"That's him!" whispered R.T. She ran down the street. Michael ran after her. Ernie was alone.

Both of the cat's eyes were closed. It looked asleep.

Ernie watched it for awhile. It didn't move. She got tired of looking at it. It wasn't a bogeyman. It was just an old, worn-out orange cat. She felt sorry for it.

Ernie was sure her eagle eye would see something. She looked at the open windows. Maybe she could see something inside. But all she could see was curtains blowing.

Ernie tugged at the walkie-talkie string. William put his cup up to his ear.

"Can you see anything?" Ernie asked into her cup.

"Nope," William said into his.

"Me neither," said Ernie. She put her cup back into her lap. She looked and looked. She ate half her sandwich. Then she looked some more.

After awhile the orange cat got up. It stretched. It yawned. It didn't have as many teeth today. It didn't stare at Ernie, either.

The cat walked to the window. It jumped inside the house. After that, nothing moved.

Ernie's bottom was getting sore. Her arms were getting tired from holding the magazine. She wished something would happen. Nothing did.

Ernie ate the other half of her sandwich. She wiggled her bottom. The stone wall was cold.

She wondered what time it was. It wasn't

afternoon anymore. It wasn't night, either. It was in between. It was probably almost suppertime.

Ernie picked up her paper cup. She was going to call William. It was time to go home.

Suddenly, she thought she saw something. Then she wasn't sure. Then she saw it again. A red glow in the window. One minute it was there. The next it wasn't. Like the glow of a fire!

Just then William tugged on the walkie-talkie. Ernie lifted the cup to her ear. She didn't need to. William was shouting.

"In the garden! In the garden!" he shouted. "It's been there all day. I just didn't see it!"

"Didn't see *what*?" Ernie shouted back.

"The bone!"

William was racing toward her. It was no good telling him to pick up the bone. Ernie would have to get it herself.

She dropped her magazine. She dropped

her paper cup. She dropped the poncho. Then she ran as fast as she could, before she could think about what she was doing. She ran faster than she had ever run in her life. She ran straight to the garden.

The bone was lying in the dirt. Ernie grabbed it. Then she ran back out of the yard. She didn't stop to pick up her magazine. Or her poncho. Or her walkie-talkie. She just kept running.

CHAPTER 5

A New Plan

Ernie was worried. She had seen the red glow. She had found the bone in the garden. Maybe Michael and R.T. and William were right. Maybe there was a bogeyman in that house.

Ernie put the bone on her desk. Then she sat down. It was time to put her eagle eye to work again. She stared at the bone.

It wasn't like bones she had seen before— turkey bones, roast beef bones, chicken bones, fish bones. They were all smaller than this bone. They all had meat on them, too.

This bone was dirty. It had been lying in the garden. But it didn't have meat on it.

Ernie got an old rag from the kitchen. She picked up the bone. She wiped off the dirt. The bone was white and smooth.

Ernie held it in her hands. It was not very heavy.

She turned it over. She rolled it around. She studied one knobby end. There was a hole in it. She studied the other knobby end. There was a hole in it, too. Why were there holes in this bone?

Ernie thought about it. She thought about William's rubber rabbit good luck piece. It had a hole in it, too. A hole in its head for the string so that someone could wear it.

But who wanted to wear a bone? No one wore bones. Not even bogeymen.

Ernie needed more evidence. But how would she get it? That was the big problem.

Ernie thought about her problem all night long. She was still thinking about it on Monday morning.

She thought about it while she ate break-

fast. There were no bananas today. Too bad.

She thought while she dressed. She thought while she brushed her teeth. She thought while she walked to school.

Ernie walked over to the jungle gym.

Marcie was sitting in the crow's nest. She was bouncing her yellow hair around. She was smiling her sweet, sticky smile.

"I heard something," she said. "I heard that Ernestine the Martian queen is a spy. The bogeyman is going to eat her up. Bogeymen like Martian spies."

Ernie pretended not to hear.

Michael was on the jungle gym, too. He was hanging by his knees. Ernie knew he was practicing being weightless. He was wearing his headphones, too. Ernie knew he was listening to Mission Control.

Suddenly, Ernie knew what to do. She would listen! Michael's brother had listened once. He had heard moans and groans. Would Ernie hear moans and groans?

Maybe. Maybe not. But whatever she heard, she would have proof!

"Michael," she shouted, "come down from there! I need to talk to you."

Michael came down. So did R.T. So did William. They all crowded around Ernie.

"You're here!" shouted William. He patted his rubber rabbit. "It did bring good luck," he said.

"We thought he got you," shouted R.T.

"Hooray for Ernie!" shouted Michael. "Queen Ernie the Spy!"

"Hooray for Ernie and William!" shouted R.T. "King William the Brave!"

William grinned at Ernie. Ernie grinned back. She stood straight and tall.

"Now listen," she told them. "I have a new plan. We are going to listen to the bogeyman. Better than that, we are going to tape-record him!"

"We are?" said R.T.

"Not me," said Michael.

"I won't go into that yard again," said William.

"I will go into the yard," said Ernie. "I will go alone. I will put a tape recorder under the window."

"What tape recorder?" said Michael.

"Your tape recorder," said Ernie. "I don't have one."

"Oh," said Michael.

"Okay?" Ernie asked.

"I guess so," said Michael, "but it better not get wrecked."

Just then the bell rang.

"Meet at Spy HQ after school," said Ernie.

Then they all ran into Ms. Finney's room.

CHAPTER 6

Strange Sounds

It was three o'clock. Ernie was sitting in Spy HQ. She was sitting on an orange crate. So was R.T. So was William. They were waiting for Michael.

Ralph was sitting in R.T.'s lap. He was chewing on one of R.T.'s braids. R.T. was chewing on the other one.

Finally, Michael came out. "I had to find an empty tape," he told them. "It took awhile." He handed the tape recorder to Ernie. He showed her how to work it. "It won't run all night," he said.

"How long?" Ernie asked.

"Almost an hour," said Michael.

"Okay," said Ernie. "Let's go."

The four friends walked to the old yellow house.

Michael and R.T. and William waited across the street.

Ernie ran up to the house. She ran up the steps. The orange cat wasn't there today. Ernie was glad of that.

She ducked behind the swing. She tiptoed to the windows. She put the tape recorder below them. She turned it on. Then she turned around. She stopped for a second. Something was different here. The porch swing was fixed.

Ernie ran down the steps. She ran to her friends. They all ran back to Spy HQ.

"Now what?" Michael asked.

"We wait," said Ernie.

They waited.

Michael got out his space map. He got out his ruler. He got out a red pencil. He drew a line from Earth to Jupiter. "We are still going to Jupiter," he said. "Soon."

R.T. fed Ralph some lettuce. She scratched his ears.

William drew a picture of the bogeyman. He had green ears. He had a bump on his nose. He had six arms.

"He looks like a Jupiterian," said Michael.

"He should look like a mean orange cat," said R.T.

"Or like Marcie," said Ernie.

William drew a nasty orange cat. It had one eye shut. It had a bald spot on its head.

"That's really good, William," said Ernie. "But it shouldn't look so mean. It should just look old and worn-out."

Then William drew Marcie. He got her mean smile just right.

Finally, it was time to go. The four friends walked back to the yellow house.

Ernie ran up to the house again. This time she did not feel quite so brave. Her tummy flip-flopped.

She ran up the steps. The orange cat still

wasn't there. It was a good thing. Ernie might not do this if it was there.

She tiptoed to the windows. She picked up the tape recorder. Suddenly, she heard something. It came from inside the house.

Ernie shivered. Chills ran up her back. Her heart pounded. She ran down the steps. She ran around the corner. She ran all the way to Spy HQ.

Michael and R.T. and William ran after her.

Michael rewound the tape. Then he played it. Everyone listened carefully. They didn't hear any moans. They didn't hear any groans. They didn't hear any puppies howling.

All they heard was tapping. *Tap. Tap. Tap-tap-tap-tap-tap.* The whole tape was nothing but tapping.

"What is it?" William asked.

"An animal," said R.T. "It is trapped inside that house. It is trying to get out."

"A hammer," said Michael. "The bogey-man is nailing something. I bet it's a coffin."

"I don't think so," said Ernie.

"Then what?" said Michael.

"I don't know yet," said Ernie.

She didn't tell them what else she had heard. It wasn't on the tape. Only she had heard it. It had come from inside the house. It had been very soft, but Ernie was almost sure what it was. It was someone laughing.

CHAPTER 7

The Bone

Tuesday was not a good morning for Ernie. She spilled her milk all over her homework. She knocked over the hamster cage at school. She messed up a spelling test. She just couldn't think about spelling. She couldn't think about anything except the bogeyman.

Finally, she tore a clean sheet of paper from her pad. She got out her ruler. She drew a line straight down the middle of the paper.

On one side of the line, she wrote "Bogeyman." On the other side, she wrote "No Bogeyman." Then she listed the evidence.

When she was finished, her paper looked like this.

Bogeyman	No Bogeyman
bone	swing fixed
fire	laugh
tap tap tap	

It did not look good. Ernie didn't think a bogeyman would fix his swing. She didn't think a bogeyman would laugh. But maybe he would. Ernie didn't know much about bogeymen.

Just then, Marcie turned around in her seat. She smiled her sticky smile. "I see what you're doing," she whispered. The smell of Juicy Fruit blew into Ernie's face.

"Mind your own bee's wax," Ernie whispered back.

"I'm going to tell," whispered Marcie.

"You'd better not," whispered Ernie.

"Marcie," said Ms. Finney. "Turn around. Ernie, get back to work."

Marcie stuck out her tongue. Then she turned around.

The morning dragged on. Ernie thought recess would never come. But finally it did.

Ernie went to the girls' room. Then she ran outside. The other kids were already there. R.T. and William were on the swings. Ernie headed toward them.

Suddenly, a big ball whammed into Ernie's stomach. It was only rubber. It didn't hurt, but it surprised her.

Ernie's feet slipped. She slammed onto the ground.

Ms. Finney hurried over. She knelt down. She helped Ernie sit up.

"Are you all right, dear?" she asked. "That was quite a fall."

Ernie's knee stung. She looked at her leg. A trickle of blood was running down it.

"I didn't mean to hit her," Marcie cried. "I didn't mean to, Ms. Finney. Honest, I didn't."

"Calm down, Marcie," said Ms. Finney. "I know you didn't mean to. You just run along now."

Ms. Finney helped Ernie to her feet. "You'd better go to the nurse's office, dear," she said. "Do you want me to come with you?"

Ernie shook her head. She trudged back inside. She shuffled down the hall.

That Marcie! Ernie didn't believe her for a minute. Marcie meant to hit her, all right. Ernie was sure of it.

Ernie pushed open the door to the nurse's office.

Mrs. Morrison looked up from her desk. She smiled. "Big day for scraped knees," she said. "You're the fifth. Sit down over there." She pointed to a chair.

Ernie sat down.

Mrs. Morrison cleaned Ernie's scrape. She put on some medicine. Then she taped a bandage over it. "Better?" she asked.

Ernie barely heard her. She wasn't listen-

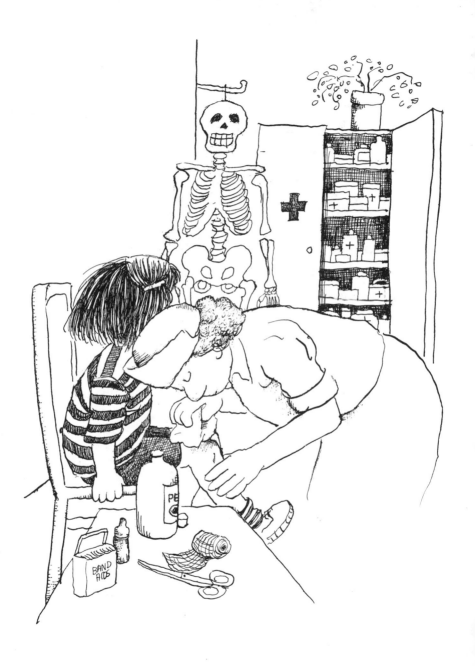

ing. She was staring into the corner. There, hanging from a metal post, was a skeleton.

"Is that real?" Ernie asked.

"The skeleton?" said Mrs. Morrison. She laughed. "No, Ernie, it's not real. It's plastic."

"Can I touch it?" said Ernie.

"Sure," said Mrs. Morrison.

Ernie walked over to the skeleton. Its bones were white and smooth. She felt one. It was not very heavy. She looked at its knobby end. It was held to the next bone with a little wire. The wire came out of holes in the ends of the bones. The bones were just like her bone—the one from the bogeyman's garden!

"Is everything all right, Ernie?" asked Mrs. Morrison.

"Thanks, Mrs. Morrison," said Ernie. "Everything is *super!*"

CHAPTER 8

Cat Power

That afternoon, Ernie passed notes to all the Martians. Each note said the same thing.

TO: All Martian Spies
IMPORTANT MEETING!
WHERE: Twin Trees
WHEN: Right after school
BE THERE!

Twin Trees meant taking the long cut home. The trees were on the way to the yellow house. They were two huge old pines. Their branches scraped the ground. They were easy to climb, but they were sticky with pine juice.

Between the trees was a secret place. It was almost like a cave. Soft pine needles covered the ground. Pine branches made green walls. It was one of Ernie's favorite places.

Ernie got there first. She sat down to wait. Soon everyone was there.

Ernie pulled out her list.

Bogeyman	No Bogeyman
~~bone~~	swing fixed
fire	laugh
tap tap tap	plastic bone

She passed it around. Then she told them about the swing and the laugh and Mrs. Morrison's plastic skeleton.

"Are you sure?" said William. "That bone sure looked real to me."

"I am positive," said Ernie.

"But who would want a skeleton in the house," said R.T. "Even a plastic one?"

"A doctor," said Ernie. "Or a nurse."

"Or a bogeyman!" said Michael.

"I would like a skeleton," said William.
Everyone stared at him.

"Weird," said Michael.

William's cheeks turned pink. "It's not weird," he said. "I would draw it. Lots of artists draw bones."

"Maybe an artist lives there, then," said Ernie.

"Gee," said William, "do you really think so?"

"But what about the fire and the taps?" R.T. asked. "What are they?"

"I don't know yet," said Ernie, "but we are going to find out."

"We are?" said R.T. "How?"

"First, we have to watch that house more," said Ernie. "Starting today. You can be eagle eyes, too. There may be a clue there."

"Bor-ring!" said Michael. "What then?"

"I don't know yet," said Ernie. "But I will think of something."

*   *   *

The yellow house was on the corner.

"You two can watch from here," said Ernie.

She pointed to the stone wall. R.T. and Michael sat down on it. They watched the front of the house.

Ernie and William went around the corner. They watched the house from that side.

There wasn't much to see. A tree in the yard. Some bushes and flowers next to the house. Lots of windows—but they were all covered.

Ernie wished she was watching the front. Then she could see the cat. This was going to be a very long afternoon.

Suddenly, there was an awful scream.

"What was *that*?" said William.

"The *cat*!" yelled Ernie. She was already running back around the corner.

By then, Michael and R.T. were screaming, too.

The orange cat was in a fight. The other cat was black. It looked like the black cat was losing. Ernie hoped so. It was the orange cat's yard, after all. Besides, the orange cat had a stiff leg and only one good eye. The black cat shouldn't pick on it.

"Do something," yelled R.T. "Somebody do something!"

"Are you crazy?" shouted Michael. "That's the bogeyman. I'm getting out of here!"

Michael tore around the corner and down the hill. R.T. and William and Ernie ran after him.

When they got to Spy HQ, William shut the door tight. "He might be after us," he whispered.

"That's silly," said Ernie. "That cat is just a sorry old cat."

"Then how come he is the only one we ever see?" said Michael. "Never a person. Just that cat. It's spooky."

"It sure is," said R.T. "And if that cat *is* the bogeyman. . . ." Her voice trailed off.

"*Then what?*" said William and Michael together.

"Well," said R.T. "He would have special power. Wouldn't he?"

"Sure," said Michael. "So?"

"I was just thinking about Ernie's knee," said R.T. "A bogeyman could have made that happen, couldn't he?"

"Of course he could!" shouted Michael.

William didn't say anything. He was shaking too hard.

"You are the spooky ones," said Ernie. "Marcie made me scrape my knee, not any old bogeyman."

"That's what you think," said Michael. "Bogeymen are tricky. I'm not taking any chances. I'm never going near that house again!"

"Me neither," said R.T. and William.

Ernie was disgusted with them. "I'm going home," she said, and she marched out the door.

"Those three," she muttered. They would never be eagle eyes. Not one of them saw the most important thing. Only Ernie had seen it.

Someone had raked the leaves. And it wasn't any old orange cat, either!

CHAPTER 9

Tap Tap Tap

For the next two days, Ernie watched the yellow house by herself. She saw the orange cat go in and out the window 6 times. She saw 17 squirrels. She saw 158 leaves fall.

But she never saw any bogeyman. She never saw a person at all.

On Friday afternoon, the weather turned cold. Room 123 went outside for afternoon recess, but they didn't stay. It was too cold.

Ernie sat slumped in her seat. It was going to be another long afternoon.

Mr. Clausen came to their room for music. Even he was boring. He taught them a new song. It was all about fixing a hole in

Georgie's bucket. Liza sang how to fix it. Georgie sang why he couldn't. Back and forth, back and forth. At the end, they were back at the first verse.

The song went on forever. It didn't make any sense, either. Liza wanted Georgie to fix his bucket with a straw. Ernie didn't get it.

Mr. Clausen had all the boys sing Georgie's part. He had all the girls sing Liza's part. Then he asked one boy and one girl to volunteer. They would sing the whole song by themselves.

Marcie's hand shot into the air. Mr. Clausen had to pick the boy himself. He picked Jo-Jo.

Brother! thought Ernie. Jo-Jo was the worst singer in the whole class.

Marcie was pretty good, though. Ernie hated to say it, but it was true. She was a good singer, and she acted, too. She tossed her head around. She put her hands on her hips. She looked just like Liza should look.

Even so, two verses were enough. Ernie didn't need to hear the whole thing again.

She pulled out her list. She added "leaves raked" to the No Bogeyman side. It was looking better for No Bogeyman. If only she could figure out the fire and the taps.

Ernie looked over at William. He sat next to her. He was bored, too. He was drawing a picture. Ernie watched him draw. It was a house. A yellow house. With a big tree in the side yard and an orange cat on the porch.

It was the bogeyman's house, but it looked beautiful. Its paint was clean. Its yard was tidy. Its shutters were straight. William had fixed it up.

Finally, the singing stopped. Mr. Clausen left.

"Take out your history books, please," said Ms. Finney. "Turn to page forty-five."

Ernie lifted her desk top.

William lifted his, too. "Ernie," he whispered. He handed her the picture. "It's for you," he said. Then he took out his book and closed his desk.

Nobody hung around after school. It was too cold. Nobody had on a warm jacket. It had been nice that morning.

Ernie ran home as fast as she could.

"I'm home!" she called.

"I'm in the den," Mommy called back.

Ernie skipped into the hall. Then she froze in her tracks.

A red light showed around the den door. It glowed. Then it faded away. Then it glowed again. Then it faded away.

Tap. Tap. Tap-tap-tap-tap-tap. Tap-tap-tap-tap. Tap. Tap-tap.

The tapping came from the den, too. Holy cow!

Ernie held her breath. She pushed open the den door.

"Hello, lamb," said Mommy. "Have a good day?"

She was sitting at the desk. The typewriter was in front of her.

"What are you doing?" said Ernie.

"Just writing some letters," said Mommy.

"What's that?" said Ernie. She pointed to a tall, skinny box. It was plugged into an outlet in the wall.

"A heater," said Mommy. "I bought it today."

Just then the heater clicked. Its tubes turned red. A red glow filled part of the room. Ernie could feel the heat.

The heater clicked again. The red glow faded away.

This was it! Everything was explained. The fire was a heater. And the tapping was typing.

"Yippee!" shouted Ernie. "I solved it!"

She raced into her room. She grabbed her warm jacket.

"I have to go to the clubhouse," she told Mommy.

"See you later, alligator," said Mommy.

Ernie headed for Spy HQ. She could hardly wait to tell Michael and R.T. and William. She had solved it! She had proved there was no bogeyman in that house.

Suddenly, Ernie stopped short. Would they believe her? William might, but Ernie didn't think Michael and R.T. would. Not after the other day.

Ernie thought a minute. Then she turned around and walked the other way. She walked straight up the hill. She turned the corner.

She stared at the yellow house. Something looked different. What was it?

Ernie smiled. The shutters were fixed!

Then she climbed the steps and rang the doorbell.

CHAPTER 10

Fried Fingers

Ernie woke up wide awake on Saturday morning. She jumped out of bed. She pulled on her clothes. She skipped to the kitchen, singing,

"Today's the day, the day, the day,
The wonderful wonderful wonderful day.
Today's the day, the wonderful day,
The bogeyman comes out."

Daddy was fixing breakfast. He was fixing French toast.

"I hope you don't need brain food this morning," he said. "I don't know how to make banana pancakes."

"That's okay," said Ernie. "My brain is great today."

"Glad to hear it," said Daddy.

After breakfast, Ernie got her backpack. Then she went to Spy HQ.

It wasn't Spy HQ anymore. The sign was gone. The *Star Finder* was just the *Star Finder* again. And the Martian clubhouse, of course.

No one else was there yet. Ernie didn't mind. She would fix her list while she waited. This would be the last time.

Bogeyman	No Bogeyman
~~bone~~	swing fixed
~~fire~~	laugh
~~tap tap tap~~	plastic bone
	leaves raked
	fire = heater
	tap tap tap = typing
	shutters fixed

Pretty soon, Michael came out. Then R.T.

came. Finally, William came too. It was time to start the Plan.

"You have to come with me," said Ernie.

"Where?" said R.T.

"To the old yellow house," said Ernie.

"No way!" said Michael.

"Ple-e-e-ease," said Ernie. "Something important has happened."

"What?" asked Michael and R.T. and William all at once.

"I can't tell you," said Ernie. "You just have to see it."

"I don't want to," said Michael. "That bogeyman is dangerous."

"You will be safe," said Ernie. " I promise. And you have to see what has happened. You won't believe it!"

"I don't know," said Michael.

"Come on," said Ernie. "We are the Martian Club, right? You are a Martian prince. Martian princes are brave."

"Well . . ." said Michael.

"Oh, come on," said R.T. "Just one more

time. I want to know what happened."

William held onto his rubber rabbit. "I won't go into that yard again, Ernie," he said.

The Martians walked up the hill. They turned the corner by the yellow house. They stood across the street.

"You can't see it from here," said Ernie. "Come on."

She held R.T.'s hand. She held Michael's hand. She looked both ways. Then she crossed the street.

William followed them. "Just up to the yard," he said, "not into it."

They stood on the sidewalk. They stared at the house.

"Where is it?" asked R.T. "The thing we are supposed to see."

"Right here," said a voice. It was right behind them.

Michael jumped. R.T. squeezed Ernie's hand hard.

A woman in a long, black cape stood behind them. She was wearing a big black hat. Her fingernails were long and red. Ernie thought she looked great.

"Eeeeek!" Michael yelled.

"Uhhhhh," said R.T.

William didn't say anything. He grabbed his rubber rabbit. Ernie heard him swallow.

"You're just in time for my breakfast," said the woman. She took William's hand. "Come into my house." She walked up the walk. She opened the door. She and William went inside.

Ernie was still holding Michael's hand. She was still holding R.T.'s hand. She pulled them up the walk and into the house.

The woman led the way. She led them into the dining room.

The table was set. There were six places. A skeleton stood behind one. It was hanging from a stand. The orange cat was asleep on the chair behind it.

"I was expecting you," said the woman.

"You sit there, R.T." She pointed to a chair. "You sit there, Ernie." She pointed to another chair. "Michael and William will sit next to me."

"How do you know our names?" asked R.T.

"I know everything," said the woman.

"Wh-wh-wh-what's for breakfast?" said Michael.

"Fried fingers," said the woman. "And stewed eyes. And toast with blood-and-guts jam."

She put plates in front of them. "Now eat!" she said.

Michael just stared at his plate. So did R.T. So did William.

Only Ernie picked up her fork. Only Ernie began to eat.

"Yummy," said Ernie. "Fried fingers are delicious."

Michael and R.T. and William stared at her. Their mouths were wide open.

"So are stewed eyes," said Ernie. "Please

70

pass the blood-and-guts jam." Ernie spread blood-and-guts jam on her toast. Then she took a bite. "Mmmm," she said. "This food is fit for a Martian queen."

Michael's eyes got bigger and bigger. R.T. chewed on her braid. Ernie thought she might chew it right off. William's hand was turning white. He was holding onto his rabbit that hard.

Ernie couldn't stand it anymore. She just had to laugh. First it was a giggle. Then it was a snort. Then Ernie gave in. She laughed and laughed and laughed. She laughed so hard her sides hurt.

The woman was laughing, too.

"We got you!" Ernie cried.

"We sure did!" said the woman.

"Her name is Kathryn," said Ernie. "We can call her Kate."

"How do you do," said Kate. "I'm very pleased to meet you."

"She's a writer," said Ernie. "The tapping was Kate typing."

"I write mysteries," said Kate. "That's why I have a skeleton. His name is Henry. I wondered where his bone went. It must have fallen off when I moved in."

Ernie took the bone from her backpack. She handed it to Kate. Kate fitted it into Henry. The orange cat opened its good eye and watched her.

"What about the fried fingers?" said Michael.

"And the stewed eyes?" said R.T.

"And the blood-and-guts jam?" said William.

"Sausage links, peeled grapes, and strawberry jam," said Kate. She winked at Ernie. "They were Ernie's idea."

"Then you are not a bogeyman?" said William.

"I am not a bogeyman," said Kate.

"What about that cat?" said R.T.

"This is Douglas," said Kate. "He looks bad, but he's a sweet old thing." She scratched Douglas's chin. Douglas closed his eye and purred.

"How long have you lived in this house?" asked Michael.

"Only a few weeks," said Kate. "I just moved here."

"I thought so," said Michael. "A bogey-man lived here before you, you know."

"Oh, Michael," said Ernie. "There aren't any bogeymen in Minnesota."

"Maybe he was a Jupiterian," said Michael.

"Well, he's gone now," said William. "Ernie has proved it!"

Ernie popped a stewed eye into her mouth. She grinned. Her eagle eye had done it again.